NOISY NORA

WITH ALL NEW ILLUSTRATIONS

►ROSEMARY WELLS◄

PUFFIN BOOKS

PUFFIN BOOKS
Published by the Penguin Group
Penguin Putnam Books for Young Readers, 345 Hudson Street, New York, New York 10014, U.S.A.
Penguin Books Ltd, 27 Wrights Lane, London W8 5TZ, England
Penguin Books Australia Ltd, Ringwood, Victoria, Australia
Penguin Books Canada Ltd, 10 Alcorn Avenue, Toronto, Ontario, Canada M4V 3B2
Penguin Books (N.Z.) Ltd, 182-190 Wairau Road, Auckland 10, New Zealand

Penguin Books Ltd, Registered Offices: Harmondsworth, Middlesex, England

First published in the United States of America by Dial Books for Young Readers,
a division of Penguin Books USA Inc., 1997
Published by Puffin Books, a member of Penguin Putnam Books for Young Readers, 2000

28 30 29 27

Text copyright © Rosemary Wells, 1973
Illustrations completely redrawn copyright © Rosemary Wells, 1997
All rights reserved

THE LIBRARY OF CONGRESS HAS CATALOGED THE DIAL EDITION AS FOLLOWS:
Wells, Rosemary.
Noisy Nora / with all new illustrations / Rosemary Wells.—1st ed.
p. cm.
Summary: Feeling neglected, Nora makes more and more noise to attract her parents' attention.
ISBN 0-8037-1835-7 (trade) ISBN 0-8037-1836-5 (lib. bdg.)
[1. Behavior—Fiction. 2. Family life—Fiction. 3. Stories in rhyme.] I. Title
PZ8.3.W465No 1997 [E]—dc20 96-4275 CIP AC

Puffin Books ISBN 978-0-140-56728-1

Printed in the United States of America

The art is all new pen-and-ink drawings with watercolor, gouache, acrylic ink, india ink, colored pencil, and pastel.

for Joan Read

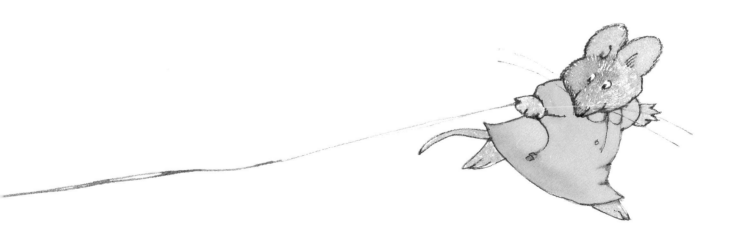

Jack had dinner early,

Father played with Kate,

Jack needed burping,
So Nora had to wait.

First she banged the window,

Then she slammed the door,

Then she dropped her sister's marbles
on the kitchen floor.

"Quiet!" said her father.
"Hush!" said her mum.

"Nora!" said her sister,
"Why are you so dumb?"

Jack had gotten filthy,

Mother cooked with Kate,

Jack needed drying off,
So Nora had to wait.

First she knocked the lamp down,
Then she felled some chairs,

Then she took her brother's kite

And flew it down the stairs.

"Quiet!" said her father.
"Hush!" said her mum.

"Nora!" said her sister,
"Why are you so dumb?"

Jack was getting sleepy,

Father read with Kate,

Jack needed singing to,
So Nora had to wait.

"I'm leaving!" shouted Nora,
"And I'm never coming back!"

And they didn't hear a sound
But a tralala from Jack.

Father stopped his reading.
Mother stopped her song.

"Mercy!" said her sister,
"Something's very wrong."

No Nora in the cellar.
No Nora in the tub.

No Nora in the mailbox
Or hiding in a shrub.

"She's left us!" moaned her mother
As they sifted through the trash.

"But I'm back again!" said Nora

With a monumental crash.

Rosemary Wells is the award-winning author and illustrator of more than sixty books for children. Her eight board books starring Max and Ruby were applauded by *School Library Journal* as "a four-star performance . . . bound to be early childhood favorites." Her *Voyage to the Bunny Planet* trilogy was called a "classic in the making" by *U.S. News & World Report*. Ms. Wells's most recent picture books starring Max and Ruby are *Bunny Cakes* and *Bunny Money*.